The Mystery
Sock Mon

THREE COUSINS DETECTIVE CLUB®

DATE DUE

AP 1 0'00			
JY 19'00			
SE 14'00			
AP 9'01			
AG 1'01			
OC 1 1 01			
JY 09'02			
JY 01 03			
FE 2'05			

F
J   Murphy, Elspeth Campbell
           The Mystery of the Sock
           monkeys

           **Three Cousins Detective
           Club #21**

BETHANY HOUSE PUBLISHERS
MINNEAPOLIS, MINNESOTA 55438

The Mystery of the Sock Monkeys
Copyright © 1998
Elspeth Campbell Murphy

Cover and story illustrations by Joe Nordstrom
Cover design by Sheryl Thornberg

Published by Bethany House Publishers
A Ministry of Bethany Fellowship International
11300 Hampshire Avenue South
Minneapolis, Minnesota 55438
www.bethanyhouse.com

Printed in the United States of America by
Bethany Press International, Minneapolis, Minnesota 55438

Library of Congress Cataloging-in-Publication Data

CIP data applied for

ISBN 1–55661–859–X   CIP

ELSPETH CAMPBELL MURPHY has been a familiar name in Christian publishing for over fifteen years, with more than seventy-five books to her credit and sales reaching five million worldwide. She is the author of the best-selling series *David and I Talk to God* and *The Kids From Apple Street Church*, as well as the 1990 Gold Medallion winner *Do You See Me, God?*, and two books of prayer meditations for teachers, *Chalkdust* and *Recess*. A graduate of Trinity College and Moody Bible Institute, Elspeth and her husband, Mike, make their home in Chicago, where she writes full time.

Contents

"Whatever work you do, do your best."
Ecclesiastes 9:10a

1

Quaint Little Shops

"*O*h, *no*! Not that! Please! *Anything* but that!"

The wails came from Sarah-Jane Cooper's visiting cousins, Timothy Dawson and Titus McKay, when she told them where they were going.

Sarah-Jane wiggled her fingers in the air and said in her spookiest Ghost Story Voice, "Oh, *yes*, my children! We are going to-o-o-o . . . the *fabric store*!"

Timothy and Titus clutched their heads and fell on the floor groaning.

"Quaint little shops!" gasped Titus.

"A fate worse than death!" cried Timothy.

The small country town of Fairfield where Sarah-Jane lived was becoming famous for the way it was fixing up its old houses. At the center of town, a row of fancy old houses had been fixed up and turned into specialty stores. A guidebook called them "quaint little shops."

Timothy and Titus couldn't even say "quaint little shops" without pretending to collapse with *unbearable* boredom.

"I see you told them," remarked Sarah-Jane's mother as she passed through the room.

"Yes," replied Sarah-Jane. "Actually, they're taking it pretty well."

Mrs. Cooper smiled down at her nephews. "That's because they remember there's another 'quaint little shop' next door to Buttons 'n Bows, don't they?"

Timothy and Titus decided not to push their luck. They got back on their chairs, looking as innocent as lambs. They knew perfectly well that the shop next to the fabric store was called Roxie's Finest Fudge.

It was a good name.

Roxie's really was the best fudge the cousins had ever tasted. You could watch it being made right there in the store. So—if you had to spend a few centuries in the fabric store in

10

order to get to that fudge . . . well, it was worth
it.

"Oh," said Mrs. Cooper as an after-
thought. "I also want to stop in at that new little craft shop, Made-by-Hand."

It was too much.

Timothy and Titus fell on the floor again.
Groaning.

2

Fudge!

"*I*'m bored," announced Timothy cheerfully before the little bell over the fabric store door had even stopped ringing.

"Ditto. Ditto. Double ditto," declared Titus.

Sarah-Jane thought about this for a moment. Much as she hated to admit it, the boys were right. The fabric store was not the most exciting place in the world.

"I'm bored, too," she said.

Her mother laughed. "Oh, all right. You kids can wait for me outside. I won't be a minute."

The cousins glanced at one another.

As if reading their minds, Mrs. Cooper

said, "I know. I know. You've heard *that* song and dance before."

Mrs. Cooper had a small sewing and decorating business. She spent *a lot* of time in the fabric store. Today she said she was just running in to put up an ad for an assistant.

Timothy, Titus, and Sarah-Jane didn't say anything. They just stared at her, trying to look like three sad little kids.

"OK, OK, you don't have to wait for your fudge," said Sarah-Jane's mother.

She got out her wallet and gave the cousins some money. Enough so that they could each get a nice chunk of fudge. But not enough so that they could eat themselves sick.

"Thank you," said Sarah-Jane.

"Yes, thank you, Aunt Sue," said Timothy and Titus. "We're outta here!"

Inside the fudge shop it was always the same thing.

The cousins would wander up and down in front of the counter, thinking hard. Considering all of the possibilities. Then they would each get the same kind of fudge they always bought.

Chocolate for Timothy.

Maple for Titus.

Peanut butter for Sarah-Jane.

The fudge was so good, it was tempting to scarf it down. But the cousins made themselves nibble to make it last longer as they watched new fudge being made.

When at long last the smell of fudge was making them woozy, they wandered outside and sat down on a bench in the warm September sunshine to wait for Sarah-Jane's mother.

The peace and quiet was suddenly broken by the roar of a motorcycle that pulled up and parked not far from them.

"EX-cellent!" murmured Titus.

"Neat-O!" agreed Timothy.

Sarah-Jane just rolled her eyes.

The motorcycle was ridden by a young man with the name *Spider* written across the back of his jacket. And he kind of *looked* like a spider. He was dressed all in black, tall and thin, with long, skinny arms and legs.

He was carrying a lumpy sack. The cousins couldn't help noticing and wondering what was in it.

The cousins were always noticing people. That was because the three of them had a detective club. They knew that good detectives had to pay attention to details. So—even when there was nothing mysterious going on—it was good to stay alert and notice things. Just to keep in practice.

That's why they noticed when Spider scowled, shoved his helmet under his arm, and stomped off.

Into the fabric store.

3

The Mysterious Stranger

*F*or a moment the cousins just sat there staring after him.

Then Timothy said, "That's funny."

"Not funny ha-ha," said Titus.

"Funny weird," said Sarah-Jane. "What's a guy like that doing in a cute little fabric store?"

The cousins looked at one another. There was only one way to find out.

Very, very casually, they got up and wandered toward the fabric shop.

So what if this was not an *actual* mystery? Keeping an eye on Spider was a good way to get some practice.

Without having to talk about it, the three cousins knew what their cover would be: three kids who were totally bored out of their minds.

Of course, that had been absolutely true the *first* time they were headed toward the fabric store. But *now* they were not the least bit bored. They were playing a detective game that was very interesting.

They had it all planned out how they would follow Spider around the store and see what he was up to without him knowing about it.

The problem was, they still had to *look* bored. And that was hard to do—to be wildly curious about something and look as if you couldn't care less.

But even the best plans don't always work out.

Spider spotted them the minute they walked in and the little bell jangled over the door. That's because he was standing at the front counter—talking to Sarah-Jane's mother.

Mrs. Cooper smiled at them but went right on talking to Spider. "Oh, yes. That's a lovely fabric. I've used it myself. But it's tricky to work with. If your aunt has any problems with it, tell her to try this. . . ."

Spider got out a notebook and carefully wrote down everything Mrs. Cooper said. Then, with a grunt of thanks, he paid for the fabric, picked up his lumpy sack, and slumped out of the store.

"What a nice young man," said Sarah-Jane's mother.

Sarah-Jane looked at her to see if she was kidding.

She wasn't.

"Ex-*cuse* me?" said Sarah-Jane.

Her mother laughed. "Well, he *is* a little unusual looking, I'll grant you that. And he doesn't say much. But here he is, on his day off, doing errands for his aunt, who has a cold."

"A day off from doing what?" asked Sarah-Jane. She couldn't imagine what kind of job a person like Spider would have.

"I believe he said he sells motorcycles," replied her mother.

Timothy and Titus gasped in awe.

Sarah-Jane rolled her eyes.

"Did you see the way he listened when I explained about that fabric?" asked her mother. "I think it's very sweet of him to be so careful to get it right. We can't always judge people by appearances, you know."

Sarah-Jane shrugged. She knew her mother

was right. People weren't always what they seemed. Detectives couldn't jump to conclusions. But still . . . *Spider?* A nice young man who did favors for his poor old aunt? Sarah-Jane had a funny feeling about it that she couldn't quite explain.

The saleslady said to Sarah-Jane's mother, "I'll leave your ad for an assistant right here by the cash register where you put it when you were talking to that—um—young man. That way, anyone who sews will be sure to see it. And speaking of sewing—I understand you're going to have some of your needlework for sale in the new craft store. Made-by-Hand is a great name for the place!"

"Yes," said Sarah-Jane's mother. "I'm really excited about it. Tonight's the Grand Opening. We haven't been inside yet, but we're headed there now. Come along, children."

"Are you talking to us?" asked Titus.

His aunt smiled and patted him on the head.

"No way out," sighed Timothy. "We'll be stuck in quaint little shops for the rest of our natural lives."

Sarah-Jane didn't say anything. That's

19

because she happened to glance out the window. Spider was a little ways off. She was surprised to see him staring back at them before he turned and hurried away.

4

Suspicions

On their way to the craft shop, Sarah-Jane's mother paused to look in some other shop windows.

Timothy and Titus groaned. But Sarah-Jane was glad because it gave her a chance to talk to her cousins. She hung back and signaled that she had something important to tell them. She looked around. The motorcycle was still in place, but Spider was nowhere to be seen. Where could he have gone?

Timothy and Titus did not seem to find the "disappearance" of Spider at all strange. Nor did they find it strange that Spider had looked back at them from outside the fabric store.

"Oh, come on!" cried Sarah-Jane. "Do you mean to tell me that you don't think Spider is the least bit mysterious?"

Timothy shrugged. "Not really. I mean, *sure*, when he first went into the fabric store I thought that was a little weird. But then it turned out that there was a logical explanation—what with his aunt having a cold and all."

"But—but—his name is *Spider*!" spluttered Sarah-Jane. "What kind of a name is *Spider*?"

"A neat-O nickname!" said Timothy. "*I* need a nickname. Something like *Snake*."

"*Snake* is good," said Titus. "I like snakes. Or *Shark*. How about *Shark*?"

"*Shark* is good," said Timothy. "How about this? I can be *Shark*, and you can be *Snake*."

"Aurrggh!" cried Sarah-Jane. "What about the sack? That's what I want to know. What did he have in that sack? Ha! Tell me that!"

"That is the *BEST* motorcycle I have *EVER* seen!" declared Timothy.

"EX-cellent!" agreed Titus. "Totally EX-cellent."

"Completely excellent," said Timothy.

Sarah-Jane sighed. Had the whole world

gone mad? Her mother thought Spider was a nice young man because she met him in a fabric store. Her cousins were so busy drooling over Spider's motorcycle that they couldn't think straight. Was she—Sarah-Jane Cooper— the only one who thought something suspicious was going on?

5

The Lumpy Sack

*T*here was no time for Sarah-Jane to argue with the boys anymore about Spider. Her mother was calling them to catch up. Timothy and Titus took a long, last, loving look at the motorcycle before following Sarah-Jane to the craft shop.

As soon as she stepped inside the door, Sarah-Jane stopped dead in her tracks. Timothy and Titus slammed into her.

There was her mother, standing at the counter talking to the manager, Mrs. Cunningham—and Spider.

Her mother smiled at them. "There you are! Come see what Spider has in his sack."

The cousins—Sarah-Jane especially—had been dying to know what Spider had in his sack. But this was almost too easy. Still, since there was no sneaky way of finding out, they decided to do the next best thing and just take a look.

What they saw surprised them.

6

Miss Marley's Monkeys

*T*he sack was full of monkeys. Not real monkeys, of course. But the next best thing. Toy monkeys. All made by hand.

"Oh, those are *so cool*!" exclaimed Sarah-Jane before she could stop herself.

"Aren't they wonderful?" agreed her mother. "I haven't seen sock monkeys since I was a little girl!" She turned to Timothy and Titus. "Your mothers and I each had one when we were little. They're so cuddly! A lady in our church made them for us."

Sarah-Jane's mother, Sue, Timothy's mother, Sarah, and Titus's mother, Jane, were sisters. Sarah-Jane was named after both her aunts.

"Why do they call them sock monkeys?" asked Timothy.

"Because they're actually made out of socks," explained his aunt. "But I've never seen any like these with their little costumes. They're just darling! Spider's aunt made them."

"I set a couple of shelves aside just for the sock monkeys," said Mrs. Cunningham. "And I made this special. What do you think?" From behind the counter she pulled out a beautifully hand-lettered sign that said Miss Marley's Monkeys.

"Oh, that's wonderful!" cried Sarah-Jane's mother. "Isn't it, Spider?"

Spider didn't say anything. He just turned a funny red and gulped.

Doing errands for his aunt seemed to make him uncomfortable, Sarah-Jane thought.

But her mother didn't seem to notice. She said, "I predict that these little monkeys are just going to fly off the shelves."

The idea of sock monkeys flying around the craft store seemed to strike Timothy and Titus as funny.

"You clowns!" said their aunt with a smile.

27

"I just meant that people are going to buy a lot of them in a hurry. And I'm going to be the first customer."

She picked up a cheerful little monkey that was dressed in a doctor's coat. He even had a little stethoscope around his neck. "Where in the world did your aunt get the stethoscope?" she asked Spider.

Spider looked as if this was the last thing in the world he wanted to talk about.

"Kid's toy doctor kit," he mumbled "Garage sale."

"That is so clever!" exclaimed Mrs. Cooper and Mrs. Cunningham together. "Please tell your aunt how much we love her work. Of course, we'll tell her ourselves when we see her at the Grand Opening tonight."

Spider grunted.

Sarah-Jane's mother said, "And tell her this little guy is going to go to a doctor's office. I have a friend who just became a pediatrician. A lot of times little kids are afraid to go to the doctor. I think if she puts this little guy in her office, the kids will feel better about being there. He's so sweet and friendly looking. Your aunt must be a very sweet person herself to make something this nice."

Spider grunted, looking like he wanted to fall through the floor.

"Anyway," continued Mrs. Cooper. "I've been wanting to get my friend a little gift as a way of saying congratulations. I couldn't find the right thing until now."

Spider grunted.

As soon as Mrs. Cooper turned away to look at something, Spider made a break for the door.

Mrs. Cunningham called after him, "And please tell your aunt that I hope her gardening goes well today. I'm sorry she couldn't come in this afternoon herself. But I'll look forward to meeting her tonight."

But Spider was already halfway outside. If he heard all this, he gave no sign of it.

7

Something Odd

Mrs. Cunningham sighed. "I do wish Miss Marley had come in herself instead of sending that nephew of hers. He's so hard to talk to. I don't even know his first name. Just goes by 'Spider.' Spider Marley if you can believe that. . . ."

"What's his aunt like?" asked Sarah-Jane's mother. "What did you say her name was? Lee?"

"Yes," replied Mrs. Cunningham. "Miss Lee Marley. I've never actually met her, but she writes a lovely letter. Very friendly but businesslike. She sent her business card. I have an extra one here. I'll put it in the bag with your monkey. Now! Let me show you around the shop!"

The cousins looked at one another in dismay. They were very proud of Mrs. Cooper's work, of course. And Miss Marley's sock monkeys were great. But—WHERE WOULD IT ALL END???

Fortunately, Mrs. Cooper happened to glance back at them. She laughed and said she guessed a little more fudge wouldn't kill them.

Sarah-Jane waited until she and her cousins were nibbling fudge in the sunshine to bring up the subject of Spider again.

The problem was, when it came to Spider, she and her cousins had a difference of opinion.

The boys liked him.

Sarah-Jane didn't.

But there was something odd she needed to talk to them about.

She said, "Don't you think it's odd when somebody lies about a little thing?"

"Who lied?" asked Titus.

"Spider," said Sarah-Jane.

"When?" asked Timothy.

"Just now," replied Sarah-Jane. "He must have told Mrs. Cunningham that his aunt couldn't come into the store herself because she was working on her garden. Don't you remember? As he was leaving, Mrs. Cunningham said to tell his aunt that she hopes her gardening goes well and that she'll see her at the Grand Opening."

Good detectives have to notice things with their *ears* as well as their eyes. And Sarah-Jane Cooper was a good detective. But that didn't mean she always got her point across right away.

"So?" asked Timothy and Titus together.

Sarah-Jane sighed. "So—he told the saleslady in the fabric store and my mom that he was shopping for his aunt *because she had a cold.*"

Timothy and Titus thought about this for a minute.

"That doesn't *necessarily* mean he lied," said Timothy.

"Right," said Titus. "I mean, maybe *both* things are true. Maybe his aunt has a cold—and she stayed home so that other people wouldn't catch it—but she still felt good enough to work in her garden."

"It's certainly *possible*," agreed Timothy.

"Sometimes the sunshine feels really good when you have a cold."

Sarah-Jane had to admit that it was possible. There was no proof that Spider had lied about anything.

And the boys had to admit that it all seemed a little odd.

8

A Little Side Trip

As soon as they got home, Sarah-Jane's mother wrote a *Congratulations* note to her friend, the new pediatrician. Then she took the little sock monkey out of the bag to box it up for mailing.

"This workmanship is just marvelous!" she said. "Not just the monkey itself, but the little coat, too. It's all so well made."

Something fluttered to the floor. Sarah-Jane picked it up and glanced at it as she set it on the table. It was Lee Marley's business card that had fallen out of the bag.

"Maybe Miss Marley could be your assistant," suggested Sarah-Jane.

Her mother looked up as if this were the most interesting thing anyone had ever said.

"Now *there's* an idea!" she exclaimed. "I'll be sure to talk to her at the Grand Opening."

Mrs. Cooper already had one assistant working for her. Her name was Sarah-Jane. Sarah-Jane didn't do any sewing or decorating. Her job was running errands. Right now Mrs. Cooper had to get back upstairs to her workshop-office. So she gave Sarah-Jane the job of taking the sock monkey to the post office.

Whenever the cousins visited one another, they brought their bikes along in case they might need them. This was one of those times.

Timothy and Titus wanted to get out and *do* something after spending all that time in quaint little shops. So they said they would go along for the ride.

After they had mailed the little sock monkey, Timothy said, "*Now* where to?"

Sarah-Jane started to shrug. Then she suddenly got the idea for an interesting little side trip.

9

A Surprise Visit

Timothy and Titus looked at her in surprise when she told them where she wanted to go.

"What do you want to go there for?" asked Timothy.

Sarah-Jane shrugged. She wasn't exactly sure of the answer to that herself. "Why not?" she said. "We told my mom we were going to go bike riding after we took care of the post office. And we're in the neighborhood. So why not?"

What Sarah-Jane wanted to do was to ride by Miss Marley's house. She had noticed the address when she had picked up the business card. It was an unusually easy address to remember: 123 Sunnyside Lane. It sounded exactly like the kind of address a nice old lady who made sock monkeys would have.

"So what are we going to do?" asked Titus. "Go up and knock on the door?"

"No," said Sarah-Jane. "I don't want to bother her. But if she's out working in the garden, we could just go up and say hi and tell her how much we like the monkeys."

"Sounds like a plan to me," said Timothy.

But—as the cousins had already discovered once that day—things don't always go according to plan.

They found the house without any trouble. But when she saw it, Sarah-Jane was disappointed. She had been expecting a kind of fairy-tale cottage with lace curtains at the windows and roses on a trellis around the door. Instead, they saw just a plain little house. It was neat and clean but not the least bit magical or even adorable.

Sarah-Jane didn't tell the boys what she was thinking. They always teased her about reading too many fairy tales anyway. And she *had* been known to let her imagination run away with her.

But then Titus raised an interesting point. He said, "If Miss Marley was gardening, she wasn't doing it in the front yard. I mean, her yard's not exactly junky, but it doesn't look as if anybody has been working on it, either."

"That's true," said Timothy. "Maybe she was working in back. But it's going to look kind of obvious if we get off our bikes and go around to check it out."

Sarah-Jane thought about this for a minute. Sunnyside Lane was exactly that—a country lane without a lot of houses. But Sarah-Jane knew if they rode on they could turn off on a side lane that circled back the way they had come. That way, they could get a look at the back of the house *without* being too obvious at all.

Timothy and Titus thought this was a good idea. It gave them some detecting practice, even though there was no real mystery to solve. Their cover would be that they were just three kids out for a bike ride.

Casually, they rode off down Sunnyside and turned onto Streamwood, which brought them around behind Miss Marley's little house.

She wasn't working in the backyard. And even from this distance, it didn't look as if anyone *had* worked there for quite some time.

So why had Spider told Mrs. Cunningham that his aunt hadn't come into the store because she was too busy gardening?

10

A Conversation With Spider

"Curiouser and curiouser," said Titus as they rode back the way they had come.

Timothy was still looking for a logical explanation.

He said, "OK. How about this? Miss Marley *plans* to work on her garden. So she asks Spider to run some errands for her. Which he very nicely did, I might add."

Timothy paused and made a point of looking right at Sarah-Jane.

Sarah-Jane made a point of ignoring him.

"So then what?" asked Titus.

"So then," continued Timothy. "Miss Marley goes out to work on her garden. But then she realizes that her cold is worse than she thought. She doesn't feel up to gardening at all. So she goes inside to lie down or something."

"You think she's in there now?" asked Titus.

They had come around onto Sunnyside and were stopped in front of Miss Marley's house again.

Sarah-Jane frowned thoughtfully. "It sure doesn't *look* as if anyone's home. You know how you can just tell sometimes?"

Before her cousins could answer, there was a loud roar, a cloud of dust, and suddenly Spider pulled up and stopped beside them.

Timothy and Titus gasped in delight at seeing the motorcycle again.

"What are you kids doing here?" Spider asked—not all that nicely.

Timothy and Titus were off in a motorcycle world of their own. So it was left to Sarah-Jane to answer, but that wasn't a problem. Sarah-Jane Cooper was not the least bit afraid of spiders or of snotty people who looked like them.

But what *were* they doing there?

It flitted through Sarah-Jane's mind to say, "None of your business." Or, "It's a free country." But just because Spider was snotty didn't mean she had to be. So she told the plain truth.

"We came to see Miss Marley."

"Why?" snapped Spider.

Why? That was a good one.

This time Sarah-Jane said the first thing that popped into her mind. It wasn't snotty, and it wasn't a lie. "We just finished mailing the little doctor sock monkey to my mother's friend, so we thought we'd stop by and tell

Miss Marley how cute it was."

Spider looked a little startled and oddly pleased. "Oh," he said. "OK." Then he thought of something else. He asked gruffly, "How did you know—uh—where she lives?"

Sarah-Jane sighed and rolled her eyes. It was getting harder and harder to stay polite. "The *business card*!" she cried.

Spider looked at her blankly.

Sarah-Jane sighed again. "Your aunt sent Mrs. Cunningham her business cards, and Mrs. Cunningham gave one to my mother. My mother has a sewing and decorating business. She needs an assistant. Someone who can sew really, really well. And she thought your aunt might be interested."

"Oh!" exclaimed Spider, sounding positively delighted.

"So—is she in?" asked Sarah-Jane. "Can we talk to her?"

"Who?" asked Spider.

"Aurrggh!" cried Sarah-Jane, so loudly that even Timothy and Titus looked up.

"Your aunt!" she exclaimed. "Miss Marley! Can we just say hi to her?"

"Oh!" said Spider. "Uh—no. She's not

home right now. She's out of town. I just came over to feed the cat."

And before Sarah-Jane could say another word, he wheeled the motorcycle into the yard and hurried into the house.

11

The Miller's Daughter

"So, gentlemen!" said Sarah-Jane to her cousins. "What do you make of *that*? Ha!"

Timothy and Titus were still staring longingly at the motorcycle. They tore their attention away long enough to look at Sarah-Jane as blankly as Spider had.

"Let's get out of here," muttered Sarah-Jane. She knew it was hopeless trying to talk to them as long as that motorcycle was anywhere in sight.

Even Timothy and Titus knew they couldn't just stand there forever. So they reluctantly got on their bikes (which by now seemed *very* puny to them) and rode along with Sarah-Jane.

"OK," said Sarah-Jane when they were

well out of sight of Miss Marley's house and Spider's motorcycle. "There's something odd going on here."

Timothy and Titus groaned.

"Oh, not *that* again, S-J!" said Titus.

"Then where is Miss Marley?" demanded Sarah-Jane.

"Miss Marley is out of town," said Timothy. "It's a perfectly logical explanation."

"That's the problem," said Sarah-Jane. "There are too many 'perfectly logical explanations.' " She ticked them off on her fingers. "First Miss Marley can't do her errands because she has a cold. Then she can't do them because she's working in the garden. Then, when we go by to see her, we find out she's out of town. Which is it?"

Timothy and Titus looked at her thoughtfully, but they didn't have any answers. Just another question. "So what do *you* think is going on, S-J?"

Sarah-Jane had an opinion, but she hesitated to share it. Even to her own mind it sounded like the opinion of someone who was letting her imagination run away with her. She took a deep breath and decided to try it anyway. "OK," she said. "Do you guys remember the story of Rumplestiltskin?"

Whatever Timothy and Titus had been expecting her to say, it sure wasn't that. Sarah-Jane could tell by the looks on their faces. She plunged ahead.

"Well, in that story, the miller has a beautiful daughter. And the miller has been bragging about her. And he gets carried away and claims that she can spin straw into gold. Well, of course, no one can do that. But the king hears about it, and he wants to marry the miller's daughter and have all this gold. So he locks her in the tower with a pile of straw and tells her to make gold out of it. But of course no one can do this. So she's crying. Who wouldn't? And along comes this weird little man named Rumplestiltskin. And he *can* turn straw into gold. So he tells the miller's daughter he'll help her but she has to give him her firstborn child. But of course, when the time comes, she doesn't want to. So he tells her she doesn't have to if she can guess his name. And he figures it's no problem for him because his name is so weird no one could possibly guess it. But she finds out what it is, and it all works out.

But that's not the point. You see what I'm getting at?"

"No," said Timothy.

"No," said Titus.

"The point is," said Sarah-Jane, "that for a while there, no one saw the miller's daughter. She was stuck away in the tower spinning straw into gold."

12

The Mysterious Miss Marley

"*I* thought it was Rumplestiltskin who was spinning the straw," said Titus.

"That's not the point," said Sarah-Jane.

"Then what is?" asked Timothy.

"That someone could be shut away someplace making stuff," said Sarah-Jane. "Only, in real life she has to do it all herself because there's no Rumplestiltskin, of course."

Slowly the light began to dawn in her cousins' faces.

"Oh, come *on,* S-J!" yelped Timothy. "Surely you're not suggesting that Spider has his poor old aunt locked away in an attic somewhere making—*SOCK MONKEYS*!"

When she heard someone say out loud what she had been thinking, it *did* sound ridiculous. But Sarah-Jane wasn't one to give up that easily.

"It could happen," she muttered.

"*Highly* unlikely," said Titus.

"OK, OK," said Sarah-Jane. "I'll grant you that it's highly unlikely."

"The most unlikely thing in the whole history of the world," said Timothy.

Sarah-Jane sighed. "Why do I even try to have an intelligent conversation with you people? At least *I'm* trying to figure out what's going on here."

"Nothing's going on," said Timothy. "You just don't like Spider, that's all. That doesn't mean that something's wrong."

"No, I guess not," admitted Sarah-Jane. It's just that . . ."

Timothy and Titus waited politely for Sarah-Jane to finish. They seemed to realize that they had gotten a little carried away just now—hooting over Sarah-Jane's theory. After all, detectives have to keep an open mind.

Sarah-Jane said, "It's just that—it seems no one's even met Miss Marley. Why not?"

"Maybe she's just really, really shy," suggested Timothy. "Maybe she's one of those people who don't like to be around other people all that much. So they just stay home all the time. What's the word for that? *Re*—something."

"*Recluse?*" guessed Titus.

"Yes, that's it," replied Timothy. "A *recluse*. Makes sense."

"It would," said Sarah-Jane. "Except Miss Marley is not a recluse who never leaves home. Spider just told us she went out of town."

13

A Wild-Goose Chase

"Oh," said Timothy thoughtfully. "Good catch, S-J."

Titus said, "If Miss Marley's out of town, I guess she won't be at the Grand Opening tonight. Too bad. It sounds silly—but I feel as if we've been off on some kind of wild-goose chase or something. It would be nice to finally *meet* this person."

"Mrs. Cunningham wants to meet her, too," said Timothy. "She's expecting Miss Marley to be there tonight. She told Spider so this afternoon. I wonder why Spider didn't just tell her that his aunt was out of town?"

"Spider didn't say anything," agreed Sarah-Jane. "He just took off."

"Oh, well," said Titus. "Maybe Miss

Marley will be back in time to make the Grand Opening."

"I hope so," said Sarah-Jane. "My mom wants to talk to her about the assistant's job."

Titus put on his best Innocent Lamb Face and said, "And maybe Spider will be at the Grand Opening, too. Won't that be nice, S-J?"

"Oh, puh-leeze!" said Sarah-Jane. "If I never hear the name of Spider Marley again, it will be too soon."

Suddenly—for a reason she didn't quite understand—Sarah-Jane knew it was very important to find out Spider's real name. The reason had something to do with something Titus had said. But she couldn't remember what that was.

"Gentlemen," she said. "I need to find a phone book."

Timothy and Titus took this announcement in stride. After all, it wasn't the first time Sarah-Jane had come up with something out of the blue. So they rode back into town and stopped at the nearest telephone booth.

"What are we looking for?" asked Titus.

"We need to look up *Marley*," said Sarah-Jane. "I need to know Spider's real name."

"Why?" asked Timothy.

"I don't know," said Sarah-Jane.

Timothy and Titus took this in stride, too. Together the three detective cousins looked up the name *Marley* in the little Fairfield phone book. There was only one listing.

It said *Marley, Lee. 123 Sunnyside Lane.*

14

An Important Phone Call

"*I* don't get it," said Titus. "It just has a listing for Miss Marley. What about Spider?"

"Maybe he has an unlisted number," said Timothy. "If that's the case, he wouldn't be in the book."

"Then how would people get in touch with him?" asked Titus. "Wait a minute! He told Aunt Sue he sold motorcycles. How many motorcycle shops could there be around Fairfield?"

They looked it up in the phone book and found there was just one.

"So now what?" asked Timothy. "Do we call up and ask to talk to Spider? What will we say when he comes to the phone?"

"He won't come to the phone," said Sarah-Jane. "It's his day off. Remember?"

"Then why are we calling and asking to talk to Spider Marley?" asked Titus.

"We're not," said Sarah-Jane. "We're calling and asking to talk to *Lee* Marley."

Timothy and Titus stared at her.

"*Miss* Marley?" said Timothy.

"What would Miss Marley be doing at a motorcycle shop?" asked Titus.

"Just trust me on this one," said Sarah-Jane.

They dug in their pockets for change, and Timothy volunteered to make the call.

"Well?" cried Sarah-Jane and Titus after Timothy said thank-you and hung up the phone. "What did they say? What did they say?"

"They said it's his day off today," replied Timothy.

15

The T.C.D.C.

Sarah-Jane called her mother and asked if she could meet them at Miss Marley's house.

Sometimes Mrs. Cooper didn't ask a lot of questions, and this was one of those times. But by the time she met them at the little house, she was dying of curiosity. "What's up?" she asked.

"Well," said Sarah-Jane as she marched up the walk and knocked on the door. "I think it's time we all met the person who made the sock monkeys."

When Spider answered the door, Sarah-Jane said, "Hi! I was just wondering if your real name is Lee."

Spider stared at her in astonishment.

Sarah-Jane continued cheerfully. "You

know, the name *Lee* can work for either a boy or a girl. I was just wondering if you were named after your aunt. I was named after both my aunts."

"Um—well," said Spider.

"I don't think you were named after your aunt," said Sarah-Jane. "Because you don't have an aunt. There is no Miss Lee Marley, is there? There is only you—Lee Marley."

Mrs. Cooper gasped. "Sarah-Jane! Of all the things to say!"

But Spider sighed and said, "I'm sorry, Mrs. Cooper, but it's true. I never meant to lie to everybody, but I didn't think people would like to buy sock monkeys made by a guy named Spider who sells motorcycles. So I sort of made up an aunt—a nice lady who sews. And that's another thing—I didn't think my friends would ever let me live it down if they knew I made cuddly toys. But I *love* to sew!"

"And you're very good at it!" said Sarah-Jane's mother, who seemed to be taking this all very well. "It wasn't right to lie, of course. But I think if you explain to Mrs. Cunningham, she will understand."

"Yes," said Timothy. "And all she has to do

is cut off the *Miss* part of the sign. So it will just say *Marley's Monkeys*."

Spider grinned at him. And Sarah-Jane thought how nice Spider looked when he smiled.

He turned to her mother. "I saw the ad you put in the fabric store for an assistant. I almost came back in and told you right there and then that there was no aunt and that I'd rather sew than sell motorcycles. But I guess I chickened out."

Timothy and Titus stared at him as if they couldn't imagine Spider chickening out of anything.

"How did you kids figure all this out?" he asked.

"Too many things didn't add up," said Sarah-Jane. "First you said one thing about your aunt, and then you said another. Ti said it was like being on a wild-goose chase. Well, the thing about a wild-goose chase is that there is no goose. And that gave me the idea that there might be no aunt, either."

"Pretty smart," said Spider.

"Well," said Titus. "What can you expect from the T.C.D.C.?"

"What's a 'teesy-deesy'?" asked Spider.

"It's letters," explained Sarah-Jane. "Capital T. Capital C. Capital D. Capital C. It stands for the Three Cousins Detective Club."

"Detectives, huh?" said Spider. "That sounds like a pretty good job."

"As good as being my assistant?" asked Mrs. Cooper. "The job is yours if you want it. I like your work, and I like you."

"We all like you," said Sarah-Jane.

"Well!" laughed Spider, looking enormously pleased. "I think we should go back to the fabric store and take down the ad because Mrs. Cooper has a new assistant."

Timothy and Titus fell on the floor groaning. "Oh, no! Not the fabric store again! Please! Anything but that!"

But Spider knew the right thing to say to get them going. "Fudge for everybody!"

The End

Series for Young Readers*
From Bethany House Publishers

★ ★ ★

THE ADVENTURES OF CALLIE ANN
by Shannon Mason Leppard
Readers will giggle their way through the true-to-life escapades of Callie Ann Davies and her many North Carolina friends.

★ ★ ★

BACKPACK MYSTERIES
by Mary Carpenter Reid
This excitement-filled mystery series follows the mishaps and adventures of Steff and Paulie Larson as they strive to help often-eccentric relatives crack their toughest cases.

★ ★ ★

THE CUL-DE-SAC KIDS
by Beverly Lewis
Each story in this lighthearted series features the hilarious antics and predicaments of nine endearing boys and girls who live on Blossom Hill Lane.

★ ★ ★

RUBY SLIPPERS SCHOOL
by Stacy Towle Morgan
Join the fun as home-schoolers Hope and Annie Brown visit fascinating countries and meet inspiring Christians from around the world!

★ ★ ★

THREE COUSINS DETECTIVE CLUB®
by Elspeth Campbell Murphy
Famous detective cousins Timothy, Titus, and Sarah-Jane learn compelling Scripture-based truths while finding—and solving—intriguing mysteries.

* (ages 7–10)